MOTHER'S HANDS

Mother's Hands

By

Björnstjerne Björnson

Fredonia Books
Amsterdam, The Netherlands

Mother's Hands

by
Björnstjerne Björnson

ISBN: 1-4101-0447-8

Reprinted from the 1897 edition

Fredonia Books
Amsterdam, The Netherlands
http://www.fredoniabooks.com

In order to make original editions of historical works available to scholars at an economical price, this facsimile of the original edition of 1897 is reproduced from the best available copy and has been digitally enhanced to improve legibility, but the text remains unaltered to retain historical authenticity.

MOTHER'S HANDS

MOTHER'S HANDS

PART I

A STIRRING clang of swords, echoing from the glass roof of the station; the ring of steel sounding through the hissing of steam, noise of laughter and talk, mingled with the dense dull sound of truck wheels, of footsteps, of luggage loading.

Every time a fresh succession of officers thronged the glass doors, the clang of swords rang sharply; many artillery officers pressed through, and some infantry among them. All were making for the door of the same railway carriage, where a tall lady in black, with large, half-melancholy, half-imperious eyes, was standing and bowing. She bent her head slowly, a measured inclination, never more. The officers evidently came from manœuvres or parade. The King was in the town, as was indicated by the presence of some of his harbingers, that is to say, Swedish uniforms. Was he here in person ? Was he expected ? No, for in that case there would have been others present besides the officers. But was that lady who stood at the carriage-door the person to whom they had come to bid farewell ? Was she the wife of a cavalry officer then ? No, that lady could scarcely have become what she was in the midst of a small military circle with horsey surroundings. Besides, there was only respect in the greeting paid to her. The crowd was round some one who was standing on the platform and who could with difficulty be seen. At that moment a white veil was waved aloft by a lady's gloved hand. Was all this parade in honour of a lady after all ?

The long prognosticated war with Russia has not yet broken out. There is probably time enough for that. Many of these officers wear decorations in advance. The colonel's manly breast bears at least eight of them. He has much to make up. Some of them—for instance, the two stately Swedes with their bland courtier eyes—are looking rather pale; perhaps they have been wounded as well as decorated in advance ?

2

The throng presses close round the carriage-door. So it is really a lady who is the object of all this bloodless fray, this pushing and pressing, this restless motion to and fro, the endlessly shifting phantasmagoria of necks and epaulettes, of features and bearded faces, this unanimous laughter to order ?

Perhaps it is a princess ? Good heavens, no! In that case they would have kept at a respectful distance ; but here they are pressing closer and closer, until the entrance doors of the station are again crowded with uniforms and clanging swords, this time exclusively of cavalry, and a little man, very old, beaming with friendliness, sheer friendliness, nothing but friendliness, appears followed by a staff of old and young officers. Discipline and Court obsequiousness (in a small army in time of peace courtiers alone are advanced to the higher grades) have made the expression of his countenance as irreproachably correct as that of an old dial-plate. Only there are moustaches on the dials which two concealed strings at the back seem to jerk now into a smile, now back to gravity again.

Some one called out, " Make room for the

general," and in an instant a wide opening was made between two saluting semicircles, suddenly parted from each other.

Then it became possible to see the centre, which was formed of a group of ladies, foremost amongst them a tall girl in a light travelling costume and a white straw hat with a long white veil floating loosely over it. Her hands were full of flowers; she kept receiving more and more, which she handed through the crowd of ladies to her mother at the carriage-door, who laid them aside. Now it could be seen by every one that the two were mother and daughter. They were about the same height, the daughter, if anything, taller than her mother; they had the same large grey eyes, but with very different expression, although both proclaimed the wide range of their inward dominion. The mother's told of a deep comprehension of the contradictions and sufferings of life, the daughter's of an ardent nature, of restless aspiration, of warring forces which as yet had not found expression; they sparkled with triumph, through which there gleamed now and then a lightning flash of impatience. She was tall, slender, supple; her

4

movements seemed to reflect the radiance from her eyes. It was not with their own eyes that others saw her, but through the light of her own. The look of energy in her face was a powerful auxiliary in the spell her eyes exercised over mankind. The mother's face was oval—of pure outline and broad design; the daughter's was longer, sharper, the forehead higher and framed by abundant light brown hair. Her eyebrows were straight, her nose was aquiline, her chin decided, her lips firmly cut. The beauty of a Valkyrie, but not so defiant. Her magnetic attraction came from enthusiasm, from impulsiveness; the flame in her eyes was light, not heat. On the whole, the impression she made was that she was borne up by invisible forces; all who came under the spell of that impression seemed to be lifted up as well. She talked to those on each side of her and in front of her, she exchanged greetings, she accepted flowers, and laughed; those who followed all these movements and changes felt dazzled and bewildered as though they had been watching waves in the sunshine.

Here was coquetry, perhaps, but with scarcely

5

a particle of the quality which singles out first one and then another. Not the faintest hint of allurement in the voice. There was no sort of enervating tenderness in that uninterrupted out-pouring of health, capacity and joyousness.

This was the reason of her success—be it said to the credit of those who surrounded her. No one came first, no one was especially dis-tinguished. They all received their meed, each after his kind.

This unanimous admiration and homage had sprung into existence the previous autumn, when the cavalry colonel, who had married her mother's sister, brought her back from Paris. This persistent candidate for the favour of men and women, who neglected no one except his own wife, had since the previous autumn had no more pressing or more important duty than to introduce his beautiful niece into society. He performed this office on horseback at her side, at balls at her side, at theatres and concerts at her side; he allowed no one else to take his place. He gave riding-parties in her honour, and the whole body of cavalry succumbed; he gave a ball in her honour at which half the assembly fell victims; he took her to the officers' great banquet, and all the guests were smitten. As an old courtier he knew every move of the game; she never appeared under unfavourable circumstances or to no purpose—on this occasion, every person present had been specially invited.

As to that, they all responded as willingly as possible; but otherwise they would simply not have known of it, or the duty of the service might not have allowed them to come, or many of them would have considered it obtrusive. Now they were there by order; to an officer the feeling that he is obeying an order adds sensibly to his enjoyment. Just look at the little general's back, as he kisses her hand, brings her greetings from his Majesty and gives her the bouquet which he himself has gathered for her in the morning! Look at his back, I say; it seems made to be patted and currycombed like a horse's. As he straightens himself again, he looks as happy in the beams from her eyes as a stiff-legged dog who sniffs meat under a napkin.

I have said that those present had the feeling,

and to an officer it is an agreeable one, of paying homage to order. That his Majesty himself had approved of her was a higher consecration yet. In the winter, out on the ice, he had deigned to fasten on her skates. It is true that she was not alone in this great distinction, or in becoming a member of the Royal Skating Club. The same honour was accorded to a great number of young girls besides. But every cavalry and artillery officer present—and there were many of them standing by when he knelt to fasten on her skates—considered it a special distinction offered to *their* lady.

Supported by the infantry, they sped after her over the glittering ice, without pause or stop—the Swedes as well. It needed but little stretch of fancy to picture her leading a sortie, to see in imagination horses, artillery, powder waggons, gliding over the mirror-like surface to the sound of horns, tramping of hoofs, and neighing of horses.

But, if she had presented no other aspect than this, all her beauty, exceptional as it was, would not have accomplished what we have just seen.

No, there was more than that. She was not

a woman to be seized, caught, held fast—it was like trying to take burning fire in one's hand. "She was neither for men nor women," some said of her, and the thought spurred them on. She eluded those who were in her presence, to the absent she seemed a meteor ; if memory is itself luminous, its glow is heightened by reflection from others.

This impression was strengthened by certain sayings of hers, some of which went the rounds.

When the King fastened on her skates he said gallantly : " You have the most charming little foot." " Yes, from to-day onwards," she replied.

A jovial colonel of artillery had dissipated a fortune on his comrades, on women, and on himself. " I lay my heart at your feet," he said. " Why, what would you have left to give away?" she laughed, and gave him her hand for the polonaise.

She stopped in the polonaise before a young lieutenant, who turned scarlet. " You are one of those one could die for," he whispered.

She took his arm in a friendly manner. " Well, to live for me would probably be a bore for both of us."

She once went to the poet-in-ordinary of the regiment, a smart captain, to offer him a philippine. " Do you wish it ? " she asked. " There is one thing we all wish in respect to you," he answered, " but we can never manage to say it—what can the reason be ? " " To say what ? " she asked. " ' I love you.' " " Oh ! of course, they know that I should laugh at it," she laughed ; and offered him the half almond, and from that time they remained as good friends as ever.

But there were other kinds of sayings of hers which aroused yet more respect. A discussion was going on one day at the fireside about a certain gate which was called the " gate of truth " ; all who went through it were *obliged* to say what they thought, upon which she exclaimed : " Ah, then I should get to know what I think myself ! " One of those present said that those were exactly the words which the Danish Bishop Monrad had used when he heard of the gate. " And he was called a sphinx," added the speaker.

She sat quietly for a little while, became paler and paler, and then got up. Some time

10

after she was found in an adjoining room weeping.

A learned man said at the dinner-table : "Those who are destined for something great know it from childhood." " Yes, but they know not for what !" she rejoined quickly. But then she became embarrassed. She tried to make a better thing of it, and said : "Some know it, and others don't," and then she became more abashed, and her embarrassment gave her an irresistible charm. People like to be conscious of the presence of lofty yearnings, even though they don't betray themselves.

In a confidential circle one evening people were talking of a young widow. "She is rejuvenating herself in a new love," said one.

"No, she is rather taking up a mission, a self-sacrificing mission," said another, who maintained that he knew her better.

"Well, I don't care which it is, provided she is devoting herself to something," said the first. "It is in devotion to something outside oneself that salvation is found—call it rejuvenation or what you will."

She had been listening to this. At first she

11

was indifferent, then she pricked up her ears, and finally her attention became riveted. Then she broke out: "No, the point is *not* to devote oneself." No one replied; it made a strange impression. Had anything happened, or was it a presentiment? Or was she thinking of something special, which no one present knew anything about? Or of something great for the sake of which it was worth waiting?

That which seems a little mysterious impresses people's minds. The better principled, the higher natured among the officers conceived respect for her. The feeling spread, and bore fruit. With disciplined wills, nothing takes root more quickly than respect.

There were certainly some who saw in her "devil take me!" the finest thoroughbred in Norway. Again there were those who would "by all the powers!" have given their hope of salvation for—I dare not say for what. But there were also those who thought of the times of chivalry and saw in their mind's eye the token the lady fastened on her true knight's breast as a consecration. A glance, a word from her, a dance with her, was the token.

Her glory fell upon them, there was something
nobler and more beautiful in them from that
moment.

How many there were who tried to draw her
from memory! for she would not be photo-
graphed. It became a common pastime to draw
her profile ; some attained the greatest pro-
ficiency in the art. With a broomhandle in the
snow, with a match in cigar ashes, with skates
on the ice.

On the whole, it certainly was to the credit of
the regiment that she should be so universally and
unprecedentedly admired. Her uncle naturally
believed that he was the cause of it, but the
truth was that the way he advertised her would
have spoiled the whole thing for any one else.
She could endure the advertisement. And now
he had been put aside, without himself understanding how it had happened. He, who on
this day had organised the whole assembly, was
standing quivering with eagerness to be abreast
of the situation ; but he could not. It all went
on over his head, as though on the second storey.
He spurred himself up with exaggerated gaiety,
with abnormal energy, but he fell back, became

13

superfluous, became actually in the way. His wife laughed openly at him ; he, who when he was abroad had hidden his wedding-ring in his pocket, and was ready to do the same thing again, was left lying in a pocket himself, like an empty cigar-case.

His wife was enchanted. From the beginning she had been alarmed when his miracle of a niece was brought into the house. The ostentatious partiality with which he introduced her into society produced results which went beyond his previsions. The crowd of worshippers kept growing greater and denser ; after the episode with the King the enthusiasm rose to a kind of frenzy for a time. The rate of speed grew with the number ; the colonel struggled to keep up like a broken-winded horse.

The bell rings a second time, there is a movement in the crowd, renewed clanking of spurs and swords, waving of hands, vociferous greetings. The heroine of the hour saluted, waved farewell for the thousandth time, gay words were spoken, smiles and bows were rapidly dispensed with cheerful grace. She was quite equal to the situation ! The large, checked travelling dress, the light hat with the veil now hanging down from it, now floating in the wind, the haughty poise of the head, the perfect figure, all this stood in the sunshine of the homage round her. Surely it was into a golden carriage drawn by white doves that she was stepping? For the moment, it was no farther than to her mother's side at the open carriage-door, whence she smiled down to the colonel on one side, the general on the other, the ladies round them. Farther back still her eyes fell on all the uplifted moustaches, the light ones, the brown, the black, the dyed, the thin moustaches, the thick, the curved, and the inane, the drooping, the smartly curled. Among that melancholy and shaggy crowd a few clean-shaven faces looked like those of Swedish tenors.

"I hope you will have a pleasant journey," said the old general. The gallant horseman was too discreet to try to say anything more marked. "Thank you for the pleasure you have given us this winter, my girl!" It was the colonel's shrill voice. The bystanders should see what a fatherly comrade he could be. "Yes, I've often pitied you this winter, uncle,"

was the answer he received. " Now you must
have a thorough rest in the summer ! "

The colonel's wife laughed. It was the
signal that all the rest must laugh.

The faces turned up towards her—most of
them honest, good-natured, cheerful—almost
every one of them reminded her of some
amusing moment ; an autumn and winter of
riding-parties, skating, snow-shoeing, drives,
balls, dinners, concerts ; a wild dance over
shining ice and drifting snow, or through a
sea of light and music mingled with the ring
of glasses, with laughter and animated talk.
Not one of her recollections had anything un-
pleasant about it. All stood out clear, brilliant
as a parade of cavalry. A few proposals,
amongst others some initiated by her worthy
uncle, had vanished like a crowd of motes.
She felt a grateful happiness for what she
had experienced, for every one's goodness, till
the very last moment. It overwhelmed her,
it sparkled in her eyes, it shone in her eager
manner, it was communicated to all those who
stood beneath, and to the very flowers she
held. But a feeling of having received too

16

much, far too much, was there the whole time. Through it all a dread of future emptiness that gave her an unendurable pang. If only it were over!

The tickets were looked at, the doors shut, she came forward again to the open window. She held the flowers in one hand, her handkerchief in the other; she was crying. The youthful figure stood in the window as though in a frame, her head, with the light hat and veil, leaning out of it. Why in all the world was such a picture not painted?

Discipline forbade that any one should press forward so long as the general, the colonel, and the ladies formed a circle; each one remained in his place. Since those near the window didn't speak, all were silent. They saw her weeping, saw her bosom heave. *She* saw them as in a mist, and it all became painful to her. Could the whole thing be real?

All of a sudden her tears were dried. A compassionate soul beneath, who also felt the painfulness of the situation, asked whether they would reach home to-day, to which she eagerly answered, "Yes." Then she remembered her

17

mother and made room for her at her side, but her mother would not come forward. There was even something in the mother's eyes which as she met them chilled and frightened her. She forgot it, for the whistle took the train away from the crowd, the whole circle fell back a step or two. Greetings were exchanged with increased cordiality, her handkerchief waved, the warmth in her eyes came back. They flashed again. All that could be seen of her called greetings to them, and they to her, as they followed. Now the lieutenants and all the young men were the foremost! Now feelings of a different sort found a different expression. The clashing of swords and spurs, the colours of the uniforms, the waving of arms, the tramping of feet made her dizzy. With her body leaning far out she reached her arms to them as they did to her; but the speed soon became too great, a few reckless enthusiasts still ran along, the rest remained behind in a cloud of steam, and lamented. Her handkerchief was still visible like a dove against a dark sky.

As she drew back she felt an aching void,

but she remembered her mother's eyes; had they the same look in them? Yes.

So she tried to appear as though she were not excited or agitated. She took her hat off and put it above her. But her mother's eyes had awakened the reaction which was latent in herself, conflicting feelings surged within her; she tried to conceal them, tried to recover herself, then threw herself down, turned her face away, and lay full length on the seat. A little while after, her mother heard her crying; she saw it too, from the heaving of her back.

Presently the daughter felt the mother's glove-less hand under her head. She was pushing a cushion underneath it. This did her good, merely to feel that her mother wanted her to sleep. Yes, she longed terribly to sleep. And in a few minutes she slept.

PART II

THE river cut its way through the landscape in
long curves.   From the south bow window in
the hotel, the mother and daughter followed its
course through tangled underwood and birch
forest ; sometimes it disappeared, and then shone
out again, and at last became fully visible.
There was a great deal of traffic going on, the
hum of it reached their ears.

Down at the station, loaded trucks were
being wheeled about.   Behind the hotel were
the works, the sawmill ; smothered thuds and
blows were heard, and more faintly the roar of
the waterfall ; over everything else the shrill
sound of the planks as the saw went through
them.   This was one of the great timber dis-
tricts ; the pine-trees darkened the heights as
far as one could see, and that was very far, for
the valley was broad and straight.

"Dear, it is nearly seven o'clock. What has become of the horses?"

"I had thought of sleeping here to-night, and not starting till to-morrow morning."

"Sleep here, mother?" She turned towards her mother with a look of surprise.

"I want very much to talk to you this evening."

The daughter recognised in her mother's eyes the same expression she had seen there at the station at Christiania: and she flushed. Then she turned back again into the room.

"Yes, suppose we take a walk." The mother came and put her arm round her neck.

Shortly after they were down by the river. It was between lights, and the softened hues of plain and ridge gave one a feeling of uncertainty.

A perfumed air was wafted from wood and meadow, and the rush of the river rose fiercely to their ears.

"It was of your father I wished to speak."

"My father?"

The daughter tried to stop her, but the mother went on.

"It was here I first saw him. Did you never hear his name mentioned in Christiania?"

"No." A tolerably long silence followed the
" No."

" If I have never spoken of him freely, I had
my reasons, Magne. You shall hear them now.
For now I can tell you everything; I have not
been able to do so before."

She waited for the daughter to make some
rejoinder; but she made none.

The mother turned half round and pointed up
towards the station, that is, towards the house
which stood beside it.

" Can you see that broad roof there, to the
right of the hotel ? There are the assembly
rooms, the library, and the rest. Your father
has the credit of it; he gave all the timber.
Well, it was there I first saw him, or rather
from there I first saw him. I sat among the
people who were going to hear him ; the whole
of the ground-floor is one single room with broad
sloping galleries, and it is built after the American
fashion ; you know that your father went over
there when he had finished his studies. Come,
now, let us go on farther ; I love this path by
the riverside. I walked along it with your father
just six weeks to the hour and day after I had

first seen him, and by that time we were married."

" I know."

" You also know that I was maid of honour to the Queen when I came here. She intended going farther out towards the fjord, but first we were to spend a few days here among the mountains.

" We came here one Saturday afternoon (as you and I have to-day) and remained over Sunday. There was a great crowd of people on Sunday to see the Queen ; they knew she was to go to church. In the afternoon they all thronged to the assembly rooms to hear your father speak. I had seen the announcement of it in the hotel. The Queen read it too ; I stood at her side and said, ' I do so terribly want to go.' ' Yes, go,' she answered, ' but you must be escorted by one of the gentlemen-in-waiting.' ' Here among the peasants !' I asked, and I took measures to go alone.

" I found a seat under the gallery, but near a large window, from which I could see a long way down the road. And as Karl Mander didn't come at the right time (he very seldom did) all

23

necks were stretched to get a glimpse of him on the road; so I saw that he was to come from that direction. I looked, too, with the rest, and a long way off there were three men visible, walking arm-in-arm, one tall and two smaller, the tallest in the middle. I have very good sight, and thought at once that he could not be one of those, for they had been having too festive a time. They happened to stand still just at the moment, then they came along wavering, first to the right, then to the left. People began to whisper and titter. As the three drew nearer I felt instinctively that the tall one was Karl Mander, and felt ashamed."

"Was he drunk?"

"Yes, he was, and the others as well; and very drunk too, both the doctor and the lawyer; and the worst of it was, they were neither of them his friends or partisans. It was a trick they had played on him, for that was what people were in the habit of doing. They had undertaken to make him drunk; but they had become still more drunk themselves."

"How horrible, mother!" She wanted to stop; but the mother went on.

"Yes. I had read all kinds of things about Karl Mander—but it was a different thing to see him."

"Were you not afraid?"

"Yes. It was disgusting. But when they came near enough for me to distinguish their faces, and all the people in the crowd who could see them laughed aloud, I shook off my fear; and when they came quite close, Karl Mander appeared to me such a marvel that I absolutely delighted in him. I admit it."

"How a marvel?"

"He was the embodiment of beaming joy! Picture a whole brigade of cavalry in the maddest gallop, you would not get such a sense of exuberant delight! The powerful figure with the mighty head held these two little men, one under each arm, as though he were dragging along two poachers. And as he did so he laughed and shouted like a boisterous child. He looked as kindly and gladsome as the longest day in the year up at the North Pole. As for the others who had set themselves to make him tipsy—for, as I have told you, it was the fashionable amusement at that time to make Karl Mander drunk—he brought them alongside in triumph. He was tremendously proud of it. He was tall and broad-shouldered, in his light checked woollen suit, which was very thin and fine ; for he could not endure heat, he was foremost among the worshippers of cold water, and bathed in it, even when he had to break the ice. He held his hat, which was a soft one and could be folded up, in his left hand. That was how he was always seen ; he never wore his hat at home, and out of doors he carried it in his hand.

" A great bushy head of hair, extraordinarily thick and brown ; which at this moment was falling over the lofty brow—(yes, your brow is like his)—and then the beard ! I have never seen so beautiful a beard. It was of a light colour and very thick, but the chief peculiarity of it was its delicate curliness. It was positively beautiful in itself—as a beard seldom is.

" And then those deep shining eyes—yours are *something* like them—and the clearly cut curve of the nose ! He was a gentleman."

" Was he ? "

" Heaven ! haven't I managed to give you that impression ? "

26

" Yes, yes—but others have————" She was silent, and the mother paused.

" Magne! I have not been able, I have not wished, to shield you from all this. As long as you were a child, a young girl, I could not explain everything to you exactly as it was. It would also have led you to try to defend that which you had not yet the power to defend, and that would have done you harm. And there was something else besides.

" But now you shall know it. Since your childhood I have never given you any advice which did not come from your father. You never saw him, but all the same I can say that you have never seen nor heard anything but him. Through me, you understand ! "

" How so, mother ? "

" Well, we are coming to that. Now I must make you understand how I came to marry him."

" Yes, dear !"

" He stood there on the platform and drank down water, glass after glass. He drank the entire contents of the water-bottle and called for more. The people laughed, and he laughed. He held the water-bottle and glass in a drunken

27

grasp, and he looked up and round him, as though he was not properly conscious of himself or of us. And he laughed. But through it all I saw the godlike in him.

"A free man's open, joyous spirit, dear; unruffled self-reliance in reaching out for that which he needed. You should have seen his firm, capable hands, hardened by toil. And his face—the face of a man who overflows with all good gifts."

"What did people say?"

"They knew him, they were only amused. And he was amused. When he began to speak he had his tongue completely under control. It seemed to me that the voice was unnatural, it sounded as though it came from inward depths. But it was his natural voice. He had hardly begun when something happened. A crowd of ladies and gentlemen strolled by, among them some of the Queen's suite. We could see them from our place near the window, and he saw them too; we saw that they pointed in.

"He stopped short, turned quite pale, and drew a breath so deep that we all heard it. Then he drank more water. It was long before he could go on speaking. They all looked at him, some whispered among themselves. Up to now he had spoken like a great machine which gives the first irregular beats with pauses between. But now he rose, and when he began to speak again he was sober. I tell you he was absolutely sober. Let me tell you by degrees, or you won't understand.

"His speech—do you know to what it can be compared ? A fugue of Bach's. There was something fulminating but abundant, uninterruptedly abundant, and often so gentle ; but there was this great difference, that he often groped for a word, changed it, altered it again, and yet it was incessant, and reverberant in spite of it all—that was the wonderful part of it. An irresistible reckless eagerness and haste. One wondered if there could be more, and there was always more, and nearly always something extraordinary.

" I had often heard people described as being possessed by some force of nature, but I had never seen it. Least of all at the Court, where marked personality is rare. I was at last face to face with one. The man who stood there was *obliged* to speak——in the same way, probably, as at a generous table he was *obliged* to drink. I knew that he managed his two farms, and worked on them himself when he had time, and I imagined that I could see the giant finding relaxation in the work ; but I saw clearly that his mind would work on as actively all the same, and that head and hands would vie with each other which should weary first.

" It was of work that he spoke. He led off by a reference to the Queen.

" ' Who is she ? ' he asked ; then he answered with some kindly feeling words about her. Then he asked again : ' Who is she ? ' He replied with another inquiry : ' Does she earn her own bread ? '

" This he held was the first obligation of all grown-up human beings who had the power to do it. That was the first standard we should apply to one another.

" ' Does she earn her own bread ? Do those who are in her suite earn theirs ? '

" ' No,' he answered, ' they don't earn it. They live on that which others have earned, and are earning.

30

" 'What do they do ? Brain work ? No, they live by the brain work of others. How do they spend their days then ?

" 'In enjoyment, mental and bodily enjoyment of that which others have done and are doing. In luxury, in idleness, in social formalities, in king-worship, in travelling, in repose do they live.' At this point he kept on substituting one word for another, but made no pause.

" Their greatest exertion, he said, was to try to enjoy an additional party or an extra levee, their greatest danger was a cold or an overtaxed digestion.

" And in order that the fruit of other people's labour should not be taken from them, what did they do ?

" They opposed everything which threatened them with a new order of things. They opposed all needful changes. They opposed emancipation for those who had nothing in the world. They behaved as though society had from eternity been ordained for them, as though they could say 'Thus far and no farther.'

" You will understand that I have learnt all these ideas from my intercourse with him. I

N

could after my own fashion make all his speeches, and that more fluently; but I believe that this exchanging one word for another, and his perpetually halting over it, made the words that he finally did choose more significant. For my part, I have written down everything that happened in our short life together."

"Everything?"

"I mean everything that mattered at all. Everything, everything. He never wrote a line, he said he had no time, he despised it. And when death took him from me and from us all, what had I better to do? No—don't interrupt me—let me go on telling you! He repeated the same thought from the religious point of view. It was his way to look at the same idea from every side. He said that to-day he had been to see an old woman who said that she couldn't go to church because she had no shoes. There was no end of trouble to get her some, for the two shoe-shops wouldn't sell any on Sunday, but she got them. He saw her afterwards go to church, just at the same time as the Queen and her suite.

"And he thought, there are so many who sit

in church with wretched shoes on, and so many at home, who dare not venture to church because of their miserable shoes, or the rest of their miserable garments. Who are they who have such wretched shoes and clothing? They who have worked most, worked until they are broken with toil.

" But those who have not worked have ten pairs of shoes, they could have a thousand; and clothes too, in the greatest superfluity. He had not been to church, he said, but he knew that there they held forth as though it were the most natural thing in the world that those who had shoes should give them to those who had none. You would gather from the preaching that Jesus Himself had taught it, Jesus had come to make all men happy, and this was the best way! For it is written, ' He went about doing good.'

" But they all went home from church just as they came; and no exchange of shoes took place, nor exchange of clothing either. One went back to his superfluity of leisure, the other to his poverty and want, and those who had not been able to go at all, because they

33

were too poor, remained after the service as they had been before it.

"Such, you see, is our Christianity, he said. And *he* had a right to speak, I can tell you, because he shared his 'superfluity' with others."

"But still you live in a certain comfort?"

"Yes, in his opinion every one had a right to do so. The man who recognised that he was called on to sacrifice his comfort also should do it; but for most educated people comfort was the indispensable condition of work and help the foundation of happiness. And there was a charm of beauty about it, too, which is a rare incentive.

"No, what he demanded was that all those who could should support themselves—hear that, my daughter!—and that those who had superfluity should employ it in work which should be fruitful for others. He called that Church cowardly and shameless which did not make that demand without respect of persons."

"Like Tolstoi, then?"

"No, they were very different. Tolstoi is a Slav by birth, Ivan the Terrible and Tolstoi both of them; for these contradictions presuppose each other. The one did everything by force, the other resists nothing. The one had to crush all wills under his own in order to make room for himself, the other will willingly yield, knowing that a desire, once satisfied, dies. The Slav impulse towards tyranny, the Slav impulse towards martyrdom, the same passionate excess in both. Born of the same people, and under the same conditions.

"All the freedom *we* in Western Europe enjoy we have attained by keeping bounds, not for ourselves alone but for others. And also by resisting. It is weakness that knows no limits : strength ordains limits and observes them."

" But yet the Bible teaches——"

" Yes, yes, but the Bible is from the East too ; the Westerns act *in opposition to* the Bible. What I am saying comes from your father."

" Did he know Tolstoï ? "

" No, but what I have been saying is older than either the Bible or Tolstoï."

"Then he was a great orator ? "

" That I could hardly venture to call him ; he could not be reckoned among the prophets, but among the seers.

" Now don't interrupt me. He believed that in another hundred years to live in idleness and superfluity would be looked upon by most people as now we look upon a life of fraud and crime."

" Oh, mother, how did you feel about it ? "

" His voice seemed to surge and vibrate in my ears both day and night. A storm-cloud seemed to surround me. Not as though he thundered or commanded. No, it was his personality, and something in the voice itself. It was deep and restrained, as though from a cavern ; it came fitfully, but without cessation. I believe he spoke for over two hours. Whomever he happened to look at looked at him, and if he looked away the other continued to gaze——he couldn't help it, you understand. His eyes blazed with inward fire, he stood bending forward like a tree on a hillside. The image of the forest rose in my mind. Later, when I was nearer to him, the breath of the forest seemed to hang round him. And his skin was so clear ! For instance, that part of his throat which was not sunburnt, because he stooped. When he lifted his head, you can't imagine how pure and fair it was.

" Ah, how have I drifted into this train of

thought ? But never mind, I have drifted into it—
and I will follow it out—it takes me to your father's
side again ! O Magne, how I loved him ! how I
shall always love him !" She burst into tears—
the girl's heart beat against hers. The softened
colours of wood and plain in the uncertain light,
the strenuous roar of the river seemed to sunder
them from each other ; the surroundings were at
war with their mood ; but the more closely did
they cling together, each supporting the other.

"Magne, you mustn't ask me to put what
I have to say to you in any sort of order. I
only know the point I am aiming at.

" Yes, he was like the nature that surrounded
him, fashioned on a generous scale and rich with
hidden treasures : so much I dimly grasped.
Everything I saw was new to me, the face of
nature as well as the rest. I had travelled, but
not in Norway.

" It is said of us women that we are not able
to analyse those whom we love, but only worship
them in the abstract. But he had a friend, his
best friend ; he could analyse him ; the poet. He
was present at Karl Mander's last meeting, and
he came to me from it when your father was

dead. We talked together of everything as much as I then could. He wrote about him the most beautiful things that have ever been written. I know them by heart; I know everything by heart that has been worthily written about your father."

"Do you know what it was he wrote?"

" 'If the landscape I see around me could speak like a human being; if the dark lofty ridge could find speech to answer the river, and those two began to talk across the underwood, then you would know the impression made when Karl Mander had spoken so long that the vibration of his deep voice and the thoughts it uttered had melted into one.

" 'Halting and with difficulty, as though from inward depths clumsily fumbling for words, he always arrived at the same goal. The thought was at last as clear and lucid as a birch leaf held against the sunlight.' "

"Was it then——"

"No, don't interrupt me! 'Karl Mander often seemed to me as unlike all other people as though he belonged to a different order of things. He was not like an individual, he represented a race. He swept by like a mighty river : at the

38

mercy of chance and natural obstacles, perhaps, but ever rolling on. So was he, both in life and in speech. Neither was his voice merely individual, it had in it the reverberation of a torrent—a melancholy, captivating harmony, but monotonous, unceasing.'"

"That surely is what the sea sounds like. mother?"

The mother was as much carried away by her memories as animated in her movements, as eager in her glance as a young girl. Now she stopped.

"Like the sea, do you say? No, no, no, not like the sea. The sea is only an eye. No, dear, not like the sea; there were warm depths and hiding-places in his nature such as the sea has not. One had a sense of intimate security and comfort with him. He was capable of the most self-forgetting devotion. Listen further. 'Karl Mander was chosen,' he wrote, 'chosen as a fore-runner before the people's own time should come —chosen because he was good and blameless; his message to futurity was not soiled in his soul.'"

"That is beautiful."

"Child, can you imagine how I was carried

away? I had had a vague feeling that the surroundings of my life were unreal; here was something that was real.

"And he himself! We women do not love that which is lofty merely because it is lofty; no, there must be a certain weakness too—something that appeals to our help; we must feel a mission. And you cannot conceive how powerful and yet powerless he was."

"How powerless, mother?"

"Well, when he came—in that condition——"

"Yes, of course."

"And his way of expressing himself. He never found the right words first, he stopped and changed them even as they poured out. And, in the meantime, if he caught something up in his hand he stood there with it. If it were the tumbler—and it generally was—he grasped it tightly, and so, because of it, would keep his hand still for a quarter of an hour at a time. His personality was so pathetically simple, or how shall I express it? He was a seer, not a prophet—yes, I told you that before. But seers are quite different, they don't know themselves so well, they have absolutely no vanity. Heavens,

40

how I longed to go and take off his cuffs! One could see that he was not accustomed to wear them : some one must have told him that it would not do to make a speech from a platform without cuffs on. He had crumpled and tumbled them ; they had come unfastened, or perhaps never had been fastened ; they got in the way and slipped over his hands. He struggled with them. There was something wrong about the waistcoat too ; it was buttoned wrong, I believe, and puckered up at one side, so that it showed one of his braces— to me at any rate, where I sat looking at him sideways and with the light full upon him. Ah, that mighty creature with the stooping head ! The tears rose in my eyes. Who would not have been willing to follow him ?

" I felt as deeply as it could be felt that *he must be helped*. I did not know that I was to help him ; I only knew that he must be helped and sustained."

A rush of memory so overpowered her that she could not go on, she turned away.

41

PART III

THE daughter saw her mother in a new light. Surely this was not she who ordered and managed her house, who sent wise letters to her, with earnest, well-weighed words! How her passion had transfigured and beautified her!

"But how did you feel, dearest mother?"

"I was not conscious of what I felt. We went away from there the day after, and our next halting-place was close to his two farms. I had my wits so far about me, however, that when some of us had to be quartered out, I chose the house which was nearest his. And when the tempest within me was no longer to be resisted I wrote to him, without signing my name. I asked him for an interview. He was to meet me on the road that went through his wood, between his house and ours. I dropped the letter into his own letter-box on the road. You can imagine what a state I was in when I tell you that I had appointed ten o'clock in the evening, as I thought that then it would be dark ! I had not noticed that it was still light at that time, so far north had we come. The result was that I did not dare to go out until eleven, and then I was sure there would be no one to meet. But there he was ! Mighty and stooping, his hat pressed together in his hand, he came forward, hesitatingly, shyly, and awkwardly, glad. 'I knew it was you,' he said."

"Oh, mother ! what did you do ? "

"All at once I began to wonder where I had got the courage from ! I did not even know what I wanted with him ! When I saw him I could have turned and fled. But his wonderful gait, those long firm strides, his hat in hand, his shaggy head. . . . I felt I must see it all. And the wonderful thing he said : 'I knew it was you.' How could he have known it ? I don't remember whether I asked him, or if he saw my surprise, but he explained that he had seen me as we came away from the lecture ; he had heard who I was. It was wonderful to hear the deep voice, which for me meant something so absolutely exceptional, as though resounding from

the far future, making embarrassed excuses for
having said anything that might have wounded
me.   Before he succeeded in getting out 'wounded
you,' he stammered——'wounded the Queen—
wounded the Queen and her ladies—wounded
you !'   He had so many other subjects he might
have touched upon, and so many other themes
he might have chosen.   He could have said so
much that was good of the Queen, much that he
knew to be true ; but he had forgotten it.   So
he went on, his eyes looking into mine—trust-
ing, but commanding eyes, whose attraction I
felt.   There seemed to be an echo in the silent
wood of his unfathomable honesty.   And his
eyes went on repeating, 'Don't you believe it,
too ?'   No one can imagine how unconscious he
was of the effect they produced.   He spoke, and I
listened, and we drew nearer and nearer to each
other.   But the joy I felt, and which could not
find words—what should I have said ?   At last
it became uncontrollable—it burst all bounds.
I suddenly heard myself laugh !   And you should
have seen how, all of a sudden, he laughed with
me !   Laughed, so that the woods re-echoed !
The fishermen were just rowing past to be at

their post when the sun should rise. They
rested on their oars and listened. They all knew
the sound of his laughter. I recognised its sound
from the time when I saw him coming between
his two satellites. There was a faun in him—a
northern faun, of course, a wild man of the woods,
unrestrained, but innocent, leading two bears,
one under each arm ! Yes, something of that
kind. Not a troll, you understand, for they are
stupid and malignant."

"You say ' innocent,' mother ? How do you
mean that he was innocent, since he was so wild?"

" Because nothing harmed him. Whatever he
might have known or experienced, he remained a
great child all the same. Yes, I tell you, refined
and as aloof from evil. He had such a power of
refinement in himself that what did not appeal to
his nature was annihilated by it. It no longer
existed for him."

"Oh, mother, how was it all ? Oh, why
have you been given this experience, and not I ! "
She had hardly spoken the words when she
turned and ran swiftly away. The mother let
her alone ; she sat on a stone and waited her
return. It was good to rest with her thoughts.

She sat a long time alone, and would willingly
have sat longer; but the clouds began to gather.
Then Magne came back with a nosegay of the
most beautiful wild flowers and delicate grasses
arranged about a fir branch covered with cones,
grey-green young cones.

"Mother, he was like this nosegay, wasn't
he? What, dear mother, are you crying?"

"I am crying for joy, my child; for joy and
regret both together. One day you will come
to understand that those are the most comfort-
ing tears in the world."

But Magne had thrown herself down on the
ground by her side. "Mother, you don't know
how happy you have made me to-day!"

"I see I have, dear child; I was right to
wait; it was a struggle, but I did right."

"Mother, dear mother, let us go back to the
forest at home, to the road through our forest!
Let me hear more! It was there it happened,
then! Mother, tell me! What came next, sweetest
mother! Ah, how lovely you are! There is
always something fresh to discover in you."

The mother stroked her hair in silence,
soothingly.

"Mother, I know that woodland road on summer nights. Laura walked there with me when she was engaged, and told me how it all happened, and the fishers rode past that time too, just as we came to an opening. We hid ourselves behind a great boulder; and the thrush began to sing, and many other birds, but the thing that affected me most was the scented air."

"Yes, doesn't it? And that is why I have always thought since that the woodland scent hung around Karl. Ah, I must tell you how curiously unconscious he was—what other word can I use? We stood still and looked over the lake. 'Oh, what a longing that gives,' said I. 'Yes, a longing to bathe, doesn't it?' said he."

Magne broke into hearty laughter; the mother smiled. "Now it no longer seems so strange to me. The water was more to him than it is to us—he used to plunge into a bath at the most unexpected times: when he was not to be found in his farms or at his office, that was always where he was. It was his strongest natural craving; he loved the cold embrace of the elements, he said.

"And how he laughed to himself when he saw how I was laughing! We laughed in unison."

"Then, mother, what happened? I can really wait no longer."

"I came home just as other people were getting up. And the next night was like that one, and the next after that, and the next after that again. One night it rained, and we both walked along under the same umbrella, and that was what brought things to a climax."

"To a climax?—how?

"After once being obliged to walk arm-in-arm, we always went arm-in-arm afterwards."

"But other people, mother? Weren't you afraid of what they would say?"

"No; other people didn't exist for me. I can't remember how it all went on—it happened that one night we had sat down."

"Ah! now we are coming to it!"

"I asked to be allowed to sit down; I felt I could walk no longer. The night was glorious —silence and we two! He went on talking with his eyes looking into mine; he didn't know himself how they shone with happiness. I couldn't speak—I could hardly breathe—I was obliged to rest. And a few minutes after I sat on his knee."

" Was it he who——— "

" I cannot quite remember. I only remember the first time my arms were about his neck and my face against his hair and beard. It was rapture, something absolutely new—it was bliss. The feeling of those giant arms round me transported me far, far away. But we were there on the boulder all the same."

" Were you as though beside yourself———? "

" Yes, that is just it ! that is what it is called —but it really means being in possession of oneself, raised up to higher things. By his side I was myself twice over. That is love ; nothing else deserves the name."

" Mother, mother ! it was you, then, who sprang into his arms ! It was you ! "

" Yes, I am afraid it was I. I suppose he was too modest, too shy to begin that sort of thing. Yes, I know in my heart it was I. For life must be preserved. It was a question of nothing less. To be able to help him, to follow him, and worship him, and give myself up to him, that or nothing. I believe, too, that

49

that was what I said to him, if I did say a single word."

"Oh, you know that you said it!"

"I believe I did; but in looking back upon such moments as those one does not know whether one was feeling or speaking." She looked out into the long valley. She stood like one who is about to sing, with lifted head and open mouth, listening for the music before it sounds. But it was not so: it was the sound of bygone music that she heard.

A little while afterwards she said quite softly —the daughter was obliged to draw nearer to her, for the sound of the river swallowed up some of the words:

"Now you shall hear something, Magne; you have never heard it from me, and others are not likely to have told you."

"What is it, mother? You almost frighten me."

"At the time I met your father I was already engaged."

"What do you say? You, mother?"

"Yes, I was engaged, and was to be married; and it was my last month with the Queen.

The engagement had taken place, and was to be carried out with the highest sanction."

" But to whom ? "

" Ah, that is it ! Didn't I tell you before, that at the time I met your father I was in absolute despair ? "

" You, mother ?   No."

" I did not believe that life had anything to offer, or that I had anything to wait for.   Most girls who arrive at the age of twenty-eight without anything having happened to them, any-thing that is worth rousing themselves for, believe that nothing is worth caring about.   The age, or about that age, is the most perilous."

" How do you mean ? "

" That is when most girls come to despair."

She took her daughter's arm, which she pressed, and so they walked on together.

" I must confess it all to you "—but there she stopped.

"Who was it, mother ? "   She said it so softly that her mother didn't hear, but she knew what it was.

" It was some one for whom you have but small respect, my child.   And you are right."

" My uncle ? "

" How did that occur to you ? "

" I don't know.   But was it he ? "

" Yes, it was.   Yes, I see you don't understand it.   I never understood it myself, either.
Think of your father, and of him !   And just
about the same time, too.   What do you think
of me ? But, oh ! take care of yourself, my child."

" Mother ? "

" Well, well—*you* have a mother, and I had
none.   And I was at Court, and, as I told you,
at the perilous age when nothing seems worth
caring about any longer.   Of course I, too, had
been playing the same game that I have been
looking on at to-day, but not with your aptitude.
Yes, you may turn away your face.   I had come
to feel a certain disgust with life—for myself
among the rest—and so I went on refusing people
till it was too late in the day."

" But—with my uncle ! "   Magne broke out
again.

" We looked upon him differently at that time.
But I don't want to go into all that again now.
I will only admit that it was horrible.   So you
may think what you like about it—I mean as to
how it came about."

52

The daughter took her arm away and looked at her mother.

" Yes, Magne, we don't always do as we mean to do, and I have told you I was at the perilous age. And so you can understand how I felt when I saw your father——there was something more than pettiness and frivolity in me after all."

" But the others, mother ! How could you put it in the proper light to the others, to the Court, to our relations, to my uncle, and all his people ? Surely there must have been a fuss and a scandal that you had to hold up your head against ? "

" Wait, Magne, we will let all that alone till later. There were no ' others' at all ! Some fishermen had seen us, and they had taken measures to find out who I was. Before it was known I had gone away, and within one month I was his wife. I had fallen into the hands of a man who did things thoroughly and at once. He was too simple to conceive any other way than to go straight forward. So it took place without any obstacles."

" And what did people say ? Was it a good thing for my father——I mean in people's opinion ——that he had married you ? "

53

"You mean that he should marry a maid of honour?" she smiled. "Do you know what people said of it? Why, Karl Mander had publicly maligned the Queen—one of her maids of honour had heard him, and a month after she had eloped with him. That was about it. She had chosen the roughest man in the country. That was what people said."

"Naturally."

"A year after a tourist wrote in a newspaper that he had seen the runaway maid of honour standing at the washing-tub. Ha, ha! It was true enough for that matter. You had come, then, and it was harvest-time, and I was obliged to lend a hand. We both did."

"Mother, mother, what was he like at home? When you were together, I mean? Wasn't it perfect? It must have been the greatest and best thing the world had to give? Mother, mother, all my life I must be grateful to you for having treasured this up for me till now, for before I should not have understood it."

"Yes, isn't it so? Such things cannot be told to a child, nor to a half-grown girl. But I am not telling you, now, only for the sake of telling you. You ask how things were when we were together. Picture him to yourself first. An unselfish, devoted nature that was very little understood, by some few perhaps, in a way, but even by them not adequately. The result was that when he believed he had found sympathy, he poured himself out so unrestrainedly that people laughed at him. If he were in company he drank, or rather was made to drink, until he was tipsy, and so let his untamable nature take the bit in its teeth. Do you know—yes, I must tell you this. At a party a lady (she is now married to the captain here) set to work to draw him out for the amusement of the others. She was very bright and witty ; she appeared to be entirely carried away by him, so that she could not listen to him enough, could not question him enough, and all the while poured more and more wine into his glass. She drank with him ; she made all the others drink with him."

"Good heavens, mother ! "

"Do you know where it all ended ? In the cowhouse. They locked him into the cowhouse by himself. His frenzy of rage brought on a

55

nervous attack. She it was whom he saw from the window as he stood on the platform that day. It was then he became sober."

The mother and daughter walked on in silence.

"You knew nothing of all this at that time, did you, mother?—not until later?"

"No; if I had known it, I believe I should have gone straight up to him, taken him by the hand, and greeted him with all my heart."

"I should too, mother!"

"Since my life with him I have thought a great deal. Do you know, I believe geniuses have this characteristic of confiding impulsiveness, and therefore the people and conditions that surround them are of all the greater importance. But most important of all is it that they should have a woman's help. And, according to the nature of that help, so things go with them. Karl Mander had got into the habit of speaking in monologues. He got on best among peasants. They disturbed him least. Books, meditations, farming, bathing, and now and then an orgie, a speech, or, for preference, one on top of the other—that had been his life up to then."

"But he didn't drink, mother? There was no need for him to drink, was there?"

" No more need than for you or for me. It was simply an outburst of mere high spirits, or repressed longing for happiness. So the last time——"

"Yes, that time! Oh, why were you not there?"

" You had come to us then, my child, and I could not ; I was nursing you at my breast. The whole thing would have gone off happily, if some one at the banquet after the meeting had not been so imprudent as to propose my health ! Then he let himself go ! There was the theme of themes, and he had never unbosomed himself about it to any one ! The toast applied the match to his inward fire ; his exultant joy blazed up. He made a speech in praise of at least twenty of my characteristics, of marriage, of fatherhood. He——"

She could not go on. She sat down, her daughter by her ; they were both in tears. The roar of the river swept pitilessly past them, and yet it seemed to bring them a kind of comfort. All the tears we may shed avail nothing. It goes on its way, and nothing arrests its determined course to the sea.

Through the voice of nature the whispers of memory brought back his tragic end. It came

over them both again how, after the banquet, he
wanted to refresh himself with a bath. How
every one tried to dissuade him, but it was no
use. How he sprang in from a great height,
took longer and longer strokes out, as though
each one of them were taking him home, was
seized by cramp and sank.

"Mother, there is so much I still want to
hear about your life together?" Then, after a
moment: "Mother, you must give me that too!
Yes, you have told me so much, so very much
about it. But not just the thing I want to know
now! The love, mother, the devotion between
you both! Mother, that must have been something too wonderful to realise."

"Beyond all comprehension, my child!
Beyond all understanding! And, do you know,
the calumnies that were spread about us,
especially the miserable anonymous letters, all
kinds of meanness, it all helped. For each time
we found in each other a perfect refuge. He
was not so thin-skinned in such matters as I.
It was through me that he first came to understand them—how to manage the petty incidents
of social life. The leaders of society in this

little country are not of pure Norwegian race, but of foreign descent. A man like him could never learn to keep pace with them. But I was one of them, and, through the effect on me, he understood ! When he once was started on a line of thought you can't imagine how fast he went. He was a discoverer, an investigator by nature. But when he first rightly found out what I had exposed myself to by choosing him, ah ! how the thought of it spurred him on ! If ever any one has been rewarded here on the earth, he rewarded me. Night and day, the whole summer, the whole autumn, the whole winter, the whole spring, we were never apart. Our life was one continued flight from the outer world, but it was a flight into Paradise. He refused all invitations ; he had hardly time to speak to the people who came to see him ; he would not have them in the house. He and I, and I and he, in the big rooms, and the smaller ones, he in mine or I in his. And on the country roads, in the fields, in the mountain pastures, on the lake, on the ice, working, superintending together, together always, or if we were away from each other it was but to

meet again at the very earliest moment. But
the more we were together the more I came to
understand the wealth of his nature. What
impressed me most about him was not the flow
of ideas, it was the man himself. To fathom
his perfect uprightness, clear to the very bottom,
gave me the most glorious moments I have
known. His devotion to me—or what shall I
call it ?—was all summed up in one image—his
mighty head on my lap ! There he often rested it,
and always said, ' How good it is to be here ! ' "

And the daughter laid her head in her
mother's lap and sobbed.

It began to rain. They rose and went home
again. The little assembly house up by the
station loomed more indistinct but more inviting
through the rain. And the landscape took on a
greater harmony of tints and greater friendliness ;
the scent from the birch-trees seemed trebled.

" Yes, my child. I believe I have given you
some of his aspirations. Have I not ? She
bent down towards her face.

Instead of answering, the daughter pressed
closer to her.

They waited a moment before going on.

"You have a longing, yearning nature ; you inherited it, and I have stimulated it in you by what I learnt from him. I have put great objects, noble men and women before you. So did he ; I have plunged you into lofty thoughts, as he plunged in nature to refresh his own. I knew when I sent you away from me that I was acting in accordance with his spirit. But I knew best with what armour you were equipped : it came to you from him. And yet . . . . Magne !"

The daughter instinctively drew her arm from within the mother's and stood still. She needed to rest on her own strength, as it were.

"Yes, I see it ; that is the third time to-day. You feel that I am taking hold upon you ; and I *will* take hold upon you. It was at the party at your uncle's that you said to me, when I was going in to supper, ' Mother, you might as well keep on your gloves.' You were ashamed of my work-hardened hands."

"Mother, mother !" The daughter covered her face and turned away.

"I will tell you this, my child, that without these work-hardened hands you would not be what you are now ; if you have lived in a

61

society where it is considered shameful for a woman to have such hands, you have lived in an evil society. And to-day you enjoyed that society, enjoyed it as though you believed you yourself had attained a certain greatness in it."

"No, mother ; no, no ! "

"Yes, you did ! You may perhaps have felt a pang of conscience or of fear ; that may be, for I was there. But now the moment has come for you to choose ; I wanted your choice to be made before you should cross the threshold of your father's house, my child. Work—or else the other thing."

"Oh, mother, you wrong me ! If only you knew ! "

"If I can make you love your father—and I shall do all I can, and you have capacity—if I can make you really, rightly love him, then I know all that you will be able to do. We women must love in order to have faith."

www.ingramcontent.com/pod-product-compliance
Lightning Source LLC
Chambersburg PA
CBHW051932240626
47153CB00004B/1468

* 9 7 8 1 4 1 0 1 0 4 4 7 2 *